****

THE

GOLD

PRINCESS

THE GOLD PRINCESS

Copyright 1-582438601
© 2011 Archie-Stevens Enterprises
Cover Photo "Tower of Gold in Bangkok" ©Sean Pavone/Dreamstine.com

This book is dedicated to the sons, daughters, grandchildren, great-grandchildren and foster children of Johnnie and Mary Archie, Sr. of Mobile, Alabama.

Table of Contents

Chapter 1 4

Chapter 2...10

Chapter 3...15

Chapter 4...20

Chapter 5...28

Chapter 6...30

Chapter 7 34

Chapter 8...36

Chapter 9...41

Chapter 10 51

Chapter 11 53

Chapter 12 56

Chapter 13 60

Chapter 14 63

Chapter 15 70

Chapter 16 72

Chapter 1

Once upon a time in a distance land beyond the Seven Seas there were three powerful kingdoms: The Gold Kingdom, The Salt Kingdom and The Middle Kingdom. The ruler of the Gold Kingdom was King Aaron. He was a fierce warrior respected throughout all the land, and he had a heart as pure as the gold that lined the walls of the mountains and covered the streams that surrounded his kingdom.

To meet him in battle none would guess the state of his heart due to his intense brown eyes, hawkish nose and his great height. He had a strong and powerful body with large tan colored hands that he used to beat down his enemies before him. The huge sword and battleaxe that he carried at his side enabled him to kill hundreds of men in any battle.

King Aaron's lifemate was Queen Adama. She was very beautiful to behold. The love that they shared was powerful and had endured much and was well-known throughout the land. The royal couple had six beautiful daughters.

The fairest of them all was their youngest, Princess Naima. With her ebony skin, doe shaped golden colored eyes, long thick curly black eyelashes, a beautiful pert nose, full brown lips, waist length black hair and a delightful personality...she enchanted all who met her.

The Gold Kingdom gleamed with gold and the roads were paved in gold and semi-precious metals. The royal palace was built using gold and diamonds, and even the pebbles on the ground were gold. The Kingdom was a glorious sight to see, but especially when the sun appeared, it was radiant. So much so that on the brightest days of the year the citizens of the Kingdom and the frequent visitors that traveled to and from the Gold Kingdom would have to wear protective eye covering.

Yet, the Gold Kingdom lacked one very important

commodity, salt. So, they traded with the Salt Kingdom. The ruler of the Salt Kingdom was King Jordan. He was known for his wisdom. Ruggedly handsome with kindness and intelligence flowing from his almond shaped dark-colored eyes, leaders of men and rulers of nations often turned to him for guidance.

The Salt Kingdom was a mountainous region. All of the houses in the kingdom were built within mountains, and the royal palace was carved from one of the largest mountains. Although King Jordan's kingdom did not have the great wealth of the Gold Kingdom, his kingdom did have something everyone needed, salt.

So, he was filled with pride when his eldest son, Prince Dalmar had asked for Princess Emon's hand in marriage. And the King of the Gold Kingdom had accepted his petition over the many other marriage offers that he had received for his lovely daughter.

The alliance between the two kingdoms would

solidify their trade relationship. And, the three hundred wagons of gold coins that were given to each of the daughters of King Aaron as marriage dowries would add to the wealth of the Salt Kingdom. Prince Dalmar and Princess Emon truly loved each other, which made it a good arrangement for all!

The Middle Kingdom sat on a large island in the middle of a great lake, surrounded by majestic mountains. It had no precious jewels and no salt, but the ruler of the Middle Kingdom, was known for his fairness and his extraordinary negotiating skills. He had the uncanny ability to broker any deal, and his kingdom had the best trained warriors of all three kingdoms.

King Oba was a handsome man with skin of ivory, chocolate brown eyes, thick eyebrows, long black eyelashes, a cherubic nose, salt and pepper-colored hair, and a well-groomed beard and moustache. King Oba often negotiated deals for his warriors to provide escort for the salt and gold traders between the neighboring kingdoms. Also, he was very good at securing successful marriage contracts between the aristocrats in all three kingdoms. For this reason, King Oba was adored by almost all the women throughout the three kingdoms.

Each Kingdom had great wealth, but the riches of the Gold Kingdom were greater than all the kingdoms in the land. Despite that fact, the three kingdoms had been at peace for over a thousand years. But, all of this would soon change because of the greed of one man, the murder of a king and the vengeance of a sorceress.

All three kingdoms were coming together for the wedding celebration of King Aaron's fifth daughter to King Jordan's eldest son. Unfortunately, King Oba had become ill and could not travel to the Gold Kingdom for the wedding celebration. So, he sent his half-brother Prince Kayan and his two nephews, Prince Chumbe and Prince Zareb in his stead. Great wickedness and immeasurable change was on its way to this land of peace and happiness.

Chapter 2

It had begun several days before Prince Kayan and his sons had left to travel to the Gold Kingdom. King Oba, though a slender man, loved to eat and to have his cooks prepare exotic dishes from foreign lands he had visited. It had been quite easy for Prince Kayan's wife to put a slow acting poison in the King's food. Since the exotic dishes placed before him were new to him, he did not note the peculiar taste.

Prince Kayan's wife, Princess Zara, was an incredibly beautiful woman with auburn hair, emerald eyes, high cheek bones, full pink lips and glowing skin. She was also very vain and thought herself to be the most beautiful woman in the three kingdoms.

Although she was greatly admired for her beauty, her beauty was overshadowed by her wicked ways. Evil filled her thoughts and her dreams were consumed by plots to overthrow King Oba so that her husband could become king. She was sure that once Prince Kayan ascended to the throne, she would be in a better position to start a war between the Gold and Salt Kingdoms.

Princess Zara hated King Aaron for his rejection of her so many years ago. Great would be her joy when he fell from power. If the two kingdoms went to war against each other, many of their warriors would die.

After that occurred the warriors from the Middle Kingdom would be able to go in and kill off any remaining warriors, except for those who would swear their allegiance to them. Prince Kayan and she would be the rulers of all three kingdoms. Those were her plans, but things would have worked out far better for her had she communicated them to her husband.

Little did she did not know that her husband, with his cold and calculating nature, had similar thoughts about overthrowing both kingdoms and gaining control over all.

A couple of days before leaving for the wedding, Prince

Kayan had sent for a creature that had been banished from the kingdom many years ago for murders she had committed.

She was the last of the Ancient Sorcerers. She was the Sorceress Aza. She was tall, incredibly thin and bony with large blue eyes and crooked black teeth. She had a purple tongue, an unnaturally shaped mouth, an overly large nose, and a perfect mixture of long flowing greenish brown hair with matching eyebrows.

She was a strange sight to see. So much so that the parents of the Middle Kingdom had often used the Sorceress' appearance as a means of frightening their children into doing things that children were not inclined to do. And it had always worked.

Many years ago, the Sorceress had used her magic powers to turn King Oba's pregnant wife and many of his wife's personal servants into stone statues. She had done this because of her great hunger to become queen of the

Middle Kingdom and because she felt that Queen Nalo stood in her way.

When it was discovered what she had done, King Oba tried to have her beheaded and her body burned, but his Council of Twelve had stopped him. To end the life of the Sorceress would have led to the beginning of a horrible curse that would have swept across the Middle Kingdom for the next one hundred years.

No living being in the Middle Kingdom could kill the last of the Ancients. But, an Ancient Sorcerer could be contained, but not in any ordinary prison. Bowing to the will of his Council of Twelve, King Oba did not have her killed.

Instead he had banished her into the enchanted forest. The trees of the forest obeyed the King and held her within its bounds. She could only be released from the enchanted forest when summoned by the ruler of the Middle Kingdom.

Although King Oba was not yet dead, his life force was rapidly leaving him. And the very air that surrounded the Middle Kingdom whispered "Soon!" And, the trees heard it, so when the command came, they obeyed it.

Chapter 3

In the early light of dawn, the Sorcerer had been surprised from her sleep by the noise of a group of warriors who had surrounded her small wooden and thatch hut. They had yelled for her to come out in the name of King Kayan. Hearing the name of King Oba's only brother announced as king, she thought she knew why the men had come.

King Oba must be dead and his despicable younger half brother was in charge. King Oba's brother was the exact opposite of him. Therefore, she knew that her skills in sorcery were needed, and for no good purpose. That suited her fine. She detested the good deeds that King Oba had used her magic for, like healing sick people, ending droughts and casting spells that destroyed crop eaters.

She had always thought that it was a waste of her great powers. Even in her confinement she still had to obey the commands of King Oba. But now she would be free of him. He was dead, dead, dead!

The Sorcerer had been forced to use her magic for such things because her ancestors had struck a blood-binding deal with the ruler of the Middle Kingdom more than three thousand years ago. No sorcerer could be hunted and destroyed as long as they faithfully served whoever ruled the Middle Kingdom.

The deal had been signed in both parties' blood. The first king of the Middle Kingdom had negotiated that deal. And, it had held until the last sorcerer had turned the King's wife into stone.

Now, with King Kayan in control, the Sorcerer Aza would be able to show her true power and be feared and given the respect she felt was long overdue her. No longer would she be forced to live in the shadows of men. She would tower above them! Her joy was so great, that she almost, but not quite, released a smile.

The warriors chained the Sorceress' hands together and tied her to the inside of the wagon. But she didn't care about these actions and the crude remarks that the warriors made or the old wagon she was forced to travel in. Her time would come and she would make these men pay for their disrespectful treatment.

The ride through the forest passed quickly, and the Sorceress was pulled from the wagon and almost dragged into the castle. She still remembered this massive room with its icy stone floors and high arched windows. It was the room from which King Oba had passed sentence on her.

She looked around, mentally counting the guards in the room as she took in her surroundings. In this very room she had been led away in chains to live in the imprisoning enchanted forest. Now she was free and freedom felt good.

The Sorceress with her chains released, quickly kneeled before the throne of the new King. And with her long thin arms outstretched as if in prayer and her forehead touching the cold stones she asked,

'"What will you have me to do?"

19

Prince Kayan was a small man, with a hard wiry body and a large head, overly protruding ears, dark beady eyes, and thick bushy caterpillar eyebrows. He had a bold nose, and his large lipped mouth was often pulled tight as in constant anger.

His skin was as dark as a moonless night, and he had matching diagonal scars carved into each cheek of his face. The marks were marks of bravery that each male had to earn on their twelfth birthday, which on other men looked quite well. The scars did not distract from their appearance. But on Prince Kayan, the marks made his appearance match his sinister nature.

"Witch, come closer!" He commanded.

The Sorceress felt herself stiffen in anger at the slight. To be called a witch was an insult, she was a great sorceress! But, she did not let her anger show as she slowly stood and moved to stand before the little king. He beckoned for her to come closer, and she did. He leaned forward and grabbed her by her right hand and jerked her to him, she stumbled and fell to the floor.

He rose and knelt next to her, whispering into her ear. And what he whispered made them both smile. It was the Sorceress' first smile in many, many years. The very air was filled with evil! And the guards in the room paled at the sight of those two co-conspirators and the unnatural pact they must have just made.

Chapter 4

The air in the Gold Kingdom was buzzing with excitement as the warriors from the surrounding kingdoms prepared to battle for first place in King Aaron's warrior games. These games were being held in honor of Princess Emon's and Prince Dalmar's wedding. King Jordan and his wives were in attendance as well as all of his children. Many noble families were there for the wedding. It was a joyous event!

"Adia, please hurry! I do not want to miss any of the games, this is the first time father has allowed me to participate in the wedding celebration and I do not want to be late," said Princess Naima.

"Princess Naima, I know you are excited, but I have to make sure you are perfect. Your sister's wedding celebration has brought the most eligible bachelors from all three kingdoms here. This is your opportunity to see the most powerful and wealthiest men of all three kingdoms."

Princess Naima rolled her lovely golden eyes at her mocicha, Adia. "Oh, please Adia do not remind me that my time to marry is fast approaching. I want to experience some of the adventures of the world, and have stories I can regale my grandchildren with, but most of all I want to marry for love."

Princess Naima loved her mocicha Adia. She was like a second mother to her, and like a mother she was too protective and too cautious. Adia was always near her, except for the times she had managed to escape from her anxious care. As the youngest of King Aaron's and Queen Adama's daughters she had been sheltered and protected like a precious jewel. But she wanted to break free!

"Look! I am finished!" Adia exclaimed.

As Adia turned the Princess around to look at her reflection in the full length mirror, Princess Naima was shocked! She could not believe that the beautiful girl in the mirror was actually her. Not a mere girl any longer, but a woman!

Adia had braided the Princess' hair and had intertwined slithers of gold ribbons that matched her eyes throughout her hair. And, she had secured her hair into a bun at the nape of her neck. Her eyes were outlined with dark kohl and her smooth ebony skin glowed.

The white fabric of her gown was trimmed with gold beading. Gold bracelets adorned both wrists and rings covered her fingers. And the single gold chain that circled her neck held a large egg-shaped diamond, which was a perfect match to the earrings that dangled from her ears. Princess Naima could not believe that in mere hours she had become the great beauty that everyone said she was, but she had never believed.

As the Princess made her way to her mother's chamber her stomach was churning in anticipation of the games ahead. To meet so many people at one time was quite unnerving, but she knew that she would be able to do it. She entered Queen Adama's chamber unannounced and was surprised that her mother was not dressed. It looked like the Queen was on the verge of crying.

"Mother, are you feeling well?" She asked.

"Yes, my precious daughter, you look beautiful and all grown up," said the Queen. "I was sitting and thinking that by tomorrow night another one of my daughters will be leaving. And you, Naima will soon be on the same path as your sisters...starting a new life with a new family. And, soon all of my babies will be gone!" She wailed.

"Mother, Zola is heavy with her first child and your first grandchild. So, please do not cry. You will be a grandmother soon and you will be able to dote on the first of many grandchildren to follow." Princess Naima gave her mother a gentle and loving smile and said, "Come mother, let me call your mocichas to help you dress."

Queen Adama and Princess Naima made a stunning pair as they entered the King's box at the warriors' games.

All eyes turned toward mother and daughter as they took their seats. King Aaron looked at his wife and all his children lovingly.

He knew the Creator had blessed him. His subjects were flourishing, no wars, two of his daughters were happily married and Emon would be married tomorrow. His youngest princess, Naima was the most beautiful and intelligent of all his daughters and he knew he would have no problem finding her a suitable husband.

As a matter of fact he had already been approached by many potential suitors almost as soon as the wedding guests had begun arriving a few days ago. The one offer that he did not like had come from Prince Kayan regarding aligning a son of his house with Naima.

King Aaron did not trust the lying and conniving Prince Kayan. There had been too many horror stories told about his cruelty toward the people of the Middle Kingdom whenever King Oba went away to negotiate contracts and peace agreements in foreign lands. To place his sweet Naima in that household would be like sending her to live with a den of vipers.

As the games began six warriors marched out on the field in front of the King and his family. They bowed low before being paired off. The games started and the first competition began. It was a competition of strength.

Princess Naima had never witnessed the competition of strength games before and she looked on with great interest as Princess Emon's fiancé fought Prince Kayan's youngest son, Prince Chumbe.

It was an amazing sight...*mmm my future brother is a fierce fighter,* Princess Naima thought as she looked over at her sister. Princess Emon looked enchanting dressed in pink, beaming with pride and wearing a huge smile on her face as she stared at her beloved Prince.

Prince Kayan's son did not take his loss very well. Princess Naima thought that Prince Chumbe looked just as sneaky as his father. Next up was Sahansan, King Aaron's chief advisor and a powerful sorcerer, who loved to compete. He was to fight Prince Kayan's oldest son, Prince Zareb.

As Sahansan turned to face his opponent Princess Naima was able to get a better look at Prince Zareb and her golden eyes widen in surprise. She felt strangely breathless. She could not believe his appearance, she thought him to be gorgeous!

As he and Sahansan faced off he moved like a lion on the prowl. It seemed like they fought forever and neither would give up. Finally her father called a draw. Unlike his brother, Prince Zareb accepted the judgment with dignity and respect.

The crowd cheered for both men and then it was time for the next competition to start, a competition with swords. As the day drew to a close, it was discovered that Sahansan and Prince Zareb were the victors for most of the games.

"How did you enjoy today's games Naima?" Queen Adama asked.

Princess Naima gave her mother a sly look and said, "It was enlightening mother."

Queen Adama clapped her hands twice and two stern looking Goldia guards appeared at her side.

"Please escort Princess Naima to her chambers!" She commanded.

"Go back to your room and rest. Tonight the events will be long." She said as she kissed Naima on the cheek before she walked away followed by her two mocichas.

Princess Naima turned to her mocicha, and exclaimed "Adia, let us go we have much to do!"

"Princess Naima, your mother said you are to rest!"

"I will rest...eventually." Princess Naima gave her mocicha a disarming smile that did nothing to relieve the poor woman's misgivings.

Chapter 5

Earlier that day, Princess Naima had overheard her father talking to King Jordan about her marrying his nephew, Prince Earlic. A feeling of dismay had washed over her after one of her sisters had pointed him out to her. She definitely did not want her father to consider a marriage for her with him.

She had thought that he looked to be a weak and spineless boy. Princess Naima wanted to marry a man, someone like Prince Zareb...tall, handsome, brave and a good fighter. She had to find out for herself if her father was seriously considering the match.

Princess Naima turned to Adia and told her to find out where her father was and report back to her at once after she had located him. More than an hour had passed before Adia swept into Naima's room looking flushed.

"I have been over the entire palace Princess Naima and I finally located your father, he is behind closed doors with King Jordan and Prince Kayan. They are in the Ochuc room."

A panicked expression crossed the Princess' face as she worriedly gnawed on her lower lip as she paced back and forth in her chambers.

"Adia, it's urgent that I talk with my father! Stay here and do not open up the door for anyone. I do not want mother to know I have gone to see father. She will only chastise me for bothering him."

"She would be right Princess Naima! What are you up to? Why don't you just rest like the Queen told you to, your disobedience usually lands me in trouble," Adia worriedly stated.

"Adia, you will not get into trouble! I am not leaving the walls of the palace like the last time. I am just going to the Ochuc room. I will be back within the hour. You can prepare my attire for tonight while I am gone!" She ordered.

Chapter 6

As Princess Naima rushed out of her room she did not notice the two swarthy, heavily robed characters that stepped out of the shadows. Before she had made it pass the next corridor they had grabbed her and shoved her inside of an empty guest chamber.

They were so busy attempting to restrain Princess Naima who struggled bravely between them, that they did not realize Prince Zareb had quietly followed them. He had just rounded the corner when he had witnessed Princess Naima being forcibly taken into a room. Prince Zareb grabbed the first attacker around the throat, and he immediately released Princess Naima. She grabbed a small jeweled and gold vase that was near the bed and threw it at the other assailant. It hit the man, and he dropped to the rug that covered a part of the marble floor.

Prince Zareb yelled for Naima to run, but she didn't. *How dare they? To touch me? To attack me in my own home?* These angry disjointed questions swirled through Princess Naima's head as she grabbed a golden candlestick, prepared to help Prince Zareb.

He did not need her help. Prince Zareb quickly subdued the first attacker by applying pressure to his windpipe, which rendered the man unconscious. He hastily lunged for the second assailant as he attempted to get up. He made quick work of him.

"Princess Naima, go back to your chambers. Now!" He ordered.

Princess Naima had never been spoken to like that before and she was furious! But before she could say anything further, Prince Zareb said it again, "NOW!"

She quickly fled to her room and at the same time Prince Zareb yelled through the halls.

"GUARDS COME QUICKLY!"

Prince Zareb could not get Princess Naima out of his thoughts as he left the area where the prisoners were being held. He had found her to be spirited and he liked that about her character. The way she had held her ground with him had impressed him. But, he was more impressed with the fact that she did not disobey him when he had demanded that she go to her room.

He didn't like yelling at her but he didn't know if any more assailants were after her. There wasn't time to be polite when there might have been another threat to her life. He would explain that to her the next time they met. He wanted her to like him. He had seen Princess Naima earlier at the competitions and had thought that she was very beautiful. But up close her beauty left him shaken!

He knew that his stepmother, Princess Zara had told his father to ask for Princess Naima's hand in marriage for her son. Although Prince Chumbe was large for his age, he was very immature and had a spiteful nature. He was younger than Prince Zareb and fresh out of the schoolroom. Princess Zara had not cared. She was determined to get the

Gold Kingdom one way or another.

Despite being the oldest son, and the one that his father should have sought as a bridegroom for Princess Naima, Prince Zareb had not protested. But now that he had met her, the thought *I have to make her my wife* entered into his head. Princess Naima was the one for him. Prince Zareb smiled foolishly at that wonderful thought as he went in search of his father.

Chapter 7

Elsewhere in the palace Prince Kayan was having a fit when news had reached him that the kidnapping he had planned had failed and the two men he had hired to kidnap Princess Naima were being held prisoner. He could not let them be questioned. Two hired mercenaries had no loyalty. Though he had never met with them his advisor, Khalil, had, and it might lead back to him. What was he going to do?

"Think! Think!" Prince Kayan silently demanded of himself. And the answer came. He marched swiftly along the hallways and stopped in the room next to where the prisoners were being held. He moved to the wall where scones of fire were kept lit to brighten the room.

He pulled one of the scones from the wall and held it inside of a bamboo basket he had located in a far corner. Fire leaped inside the basket. Prince Kayan kicked the basket over, rolling it near the door of the room where

36

another basket sat, quickly setting it on fire.

Then he left the room, and tucked himself into a wall space near a high marble column. The smell of fire was quickly noticed, and a cry went out. The guards in the prisoners' room rushed out, and Prince Kayan slipped in and slit the throats of both bound men, and slipped out just as quickly.

When Prince Zareb heard the shouts of "Fire!" He changed directions and ran toward the commotion. The guards had already put the small blazes out by the time he had made it to the scene. He went to check on the prisoners and discovered a gruesome sight. Both of their throats had been slit!

Obviously, the fire had been purposely set to distract the guards. Icy cold fingers of fear crept up his spine because he was certain that his beautiful Princess was still in danger. He quickly turned to one of the guards and told him to send for the King.

37

Chapter 8

Princess Naima could not believe that in less than twenty four hours she had witnessed her first warrior competition. And had almost been kidnapped, and then saved by the fierce and handsome Prince Zareb. And, now she could not stop thinking about him. I am in love, she thought!

All of the nighttime events had been cancelled because of the attack upon her. And she had been confined to her chambers. She felt too restless to sleep. But, she was wrong. The excitement of the day caught her unaware and before she knew it she had drifted off to sleep with dreams filled with the daring and handsome Prince Zareb.

However there was someone in her chambers that could not sleep. It was her mocicha, Adia. She was very upset. She kept moving from her small bed in the antechamber and back into the Princess' room to stare at her as she slept. She had cared for Princess Naima from birth and had loved her as if she was her own daughter.

This evening her precious Princess had almost been taken from her. She trembled at the thought of what those men might have done to her. As Princess Naima slept, Adia prayed over her and asked the Creator to shield and protect Naima. Adia could feel evil lurking in the shadows and she felt certain something very bad was going to happen before all the events of Princess Emon's wedding celebrations had come to a conclusion.

A quiet knock at the door interrupted Adia's gloomy thoughts and she moved forward to answer. It was King Aaron and Queen Adama. Adia immediately bowed before them.

Queen Adama said, "We are here to check on Naima and to let you know to keep Naima in her rooms tonight."

"There has been more trouble, and I do not want Naima to leave her chambers until the wedding tomorrow", said King Aaron.

"I will send Sahansan to escort Naima to the wedding ceremony. In the meantime there will be guards outside the door, if you need anything they will make sure that it is delivered to this room. Have I made myself clear Adia?" he asked.

"Yes, King Aaron. I love the princess and I will die to protect her." She lowered her head and dropped into a deep bow as the royal couple left the room.

The next morning the sun seemed to be smiling down on the Gold Kingdom. Princess Naima looked out her window at the brightness of the day and the glorious colors that the people below were wearing in honor of the wedding. She was excited and a little sad. Emon was her sister and her best friend. Princess Naima knew when Emon left for her new home she would rarely get to see her.

The Princess having such a sunny disposition could

not stay sad for long as her thoughts changed to how happy Prince Dalmar and Emon seem to be. And, she knew that she would share a similar bond with Prince Zareb if she had anything to do with it. She grinned mischievously as Adia neared her.

Adia threw up her hands in mock horror and said, "Oh no, what are you up to now? I know when you smile like that you have some wild idea in your head!"

"No Adia, you are wrong this time, I am just happy. Is my bath ready? Yesterday, you made me beautiful, but today I want to be dazzling. I am going to let you in on a little secret, I am in love with Prince Zareb and I really want him to notice me!" exclaimed the Princess.

Adia set out to make her Princess shine. And she succeeded beyond both of their wildest imagination. King Aaron received more petitions for marriage to Princess Naima that day than he had in months for all of his unmarried daughters combined. He could not help swelling with pride as he received one offer after another.

He loved all of his daughters and they were all very beautiful. But today Naima appeared to glow with an inner and outer beauty that he had not noticed before, and her tinkling laughter rang out among her sisters in a delightful manner. If, he had taken the time to notice the many glances she had given in Prince Zareb's direction, he would have known why his daughter was glowing with happiness.

Chapter 9

The wedding was glorious and as Princess Naima looked around at all of the guests in the enormous marble room she was amazed at the sight. The women and children were beautiful and all the men looked handsome.

Everyone looked so happy. Princess Emon and Prince Dalmar could not stop looking at each other. Her mother and father were looking at each other like they were the newlyweds. And Prince Zareb was looking very handsome in his formal dress.

The only two people that looked like they did not belong were Prince Kayan and his son, Prince Chumbe. They reminded her of reptiles, cold blooded and repulsive. It amazed her that Prince Zareb was related to those two. She did not think he looked like his father, and he certainly did not appear to act like him either.

To Princess Naima, Prince Zareb was everything good and decent that his father and brother were not. She felt it a shame that Prince Zareb was not King Oba's son instead of Prince Kayan's son.

As the tables were being cleared, the guests began to move into the Sokiya room for music and dancing, Princess Naima could barely contain her excitement. She loved to dance. As the drummers began playing, Princess Naima felt her body beginning to sway to the beat. She and other girls of marriageable age moved to the center of the floor and began to captivate the crowd with their graceful and nimble movements.

Once the music for the Haku dance began the unmarried men could join in when the drummers increased the beating of their drums. Each man would be allowed to pick a maiden to dance beside him. It was an opportunity for the men to get a closer look at possible future brides under the watchful eyes of parents and guardians.

Princess Naima kept thinking to herself *please let Prince Zareb make his way to me*. She made sure she stayed toward the outside of the group where he would be sure to see her, but Princess Naima did not like the way his repulsive brother seemed to be inching closer to her, so she moved farther away.

Then it happened! The drum beats increased and Prince Zareb moved forward and merged in with the dancers and moved next to her. Princess Naima was glowing with excitement and her golden eyes sparkled as they moved in unison to the beat of the drums as they made their way through the steps of the traditional Haku dance.

It was a dance that had been danced at wedding celebrations in the Gold Kingdom for thousands of years. As the drum beats slowed Prince Zareb and Princess Naima turned and faced each other, their eyes met and time appeared to stand still.

Prince Zareb felt as though he could hear the beating of his heart above the tempo of the drums. He felt dazed, yet excited. It was as if he had drunk from the nectar fountain where the feast was held, but he had not touched a drop.

The swelling of emotions that raced through his blood as he continued to gaze into the Princess' lovely eyes was real and they both knew in that instance that they were born to be together. There was no other explanation for the feelings that swept over them.

King Aaron and Queen Adama looked on with interest at their daughter and Prince Zareb. They looked very good together. The King became worried as it dawn on him that Prince Zareb was the reason for his daughter unusually high spirits.

"Well my warrior king," Queen Adama laughingly said to her husband. "I think we may be planning another wedding celebration a lot sooner than expected."

King Aaron smiled at his Queen, but did not say a word. He was thinking back to a time when he had accepted an invitation to join a hunting party with King

Oba and other noblemen in the Middle Kingdom. When he had retired for the night, Princess Zara had entered his room and offered herself to him.

He had politely refused her offer at first, but when she refused to leave, he had pushed her out into the corridor and locked his door against her. He had left the island the next day to avoid coming into contact with her again. He loved his wife very much and could not think why Princess Zara had approached him.

He had never mentioned the incident to his wife, but he felt that he might have to in order to explain why he did not want any of his daughters to marry into that family. Prince Zareb had saved Princess Naima, and he appeared to be an honorable man and an excellent warrior, but his father and stepmother were…he refused to think further about it. He would just wait and see what happened.

He broke off his reflections and spoke to his wife, "I think you are right, beautiful. You know we are not too old to have more children?" He arched one brow at her and leaned in closer.

The Queen touched her husband lovingly on the cheek and said. "You are right, husband. I still want a bouncing baby boy that looks just like you." They laughed together and turned back to watch the dancers.

Princess Naima felt that she could dance forever if Prince Zareb could stay by her side, but like all things it had to come to an end. When the music stopped he asked her if she would like to sit and talk. She shyly nodded her head, yes.

He led her to a quiet corner of the huge room where they could still be seen by all and it seemed like they talked for hours.

"Your parents seem to be very much in love Princess Naima," said Prince Zareb.

"Yes, they are lifemates, no bond is stronger between a man and a woman than a life bond," Princess

Naima shyly said to Prince Zareb.

"Everyone is not so lucky to find a lifemate. My parents were not lifemates and I can remember the sadness that always seemed to lurk in my mother's eyes. My father is not a good man, but my grandparents did not know that when they arranged the marriage.

My mother died when I was nine years of age. Yet the memories of our time together are still fresh in my mind. When she died it was as though my childhood and innocence died with her." Prince Zareb did not feel strange about sharing such personal thoughts with the Princess.

"Is it agreeable to you if I call you Naima? I feel such closeness to you?" He was hoping that he was not moving too fast, but he could not help himself.

"Yes, of course you may, but only if I can call you, Zareb?"

Princess Naima was slightly shocked at herself for being so bold, but it felt natural to speak with him as though she had known him for years instead of a couple of short days.

"You make my name sound like music upon your lips. Your voice is the sweetest sound I have ever heard."

"Oh Zareb, you are making me blush! I am sorry that you have gone through so much pain in your life, but I feel that your future will be filled with happiness." She met his eyes briefly before shyly looking away.

"Naima, I have the same feeling and I think a beautiful Princess from the Gold Kingdom will play a big part in that future," said Prince Zareb. His heart was racing and his blood felt as if it was on fire. If his father would not speak to King Aaron on his behalf, he knew he would do it himself. He loved her and could not envision a life without her. Not only was she beautiful, but she had a warm and compassionate nature.

Princess Naima smiled at Zareb. But, before she could respond to his declaration, Sahansan appeared out of nowhere and stood directly in front of the love struck couple.

"Princess, I am here to escort you to your chambers."

Princess Naima was about to protest, but Prince Zareb must have noticed the look on her face because before she could protest Zareb said, "It is alright Naima, I will see you tomorrow."

As he stood up, he offered her his hand and she placed her hand in his and it felt so right to the both of them that they smiled yet again.

Prince Zareb turned to Sahansan and said, "Take good care of her."

He took another long look at her as she walked away with Sahansan. Princess Naima did not feel her slippers touching the marble floor as she walked beside the chief advisor. She felt like she was floating on air. Her life at that moment seemed like a wonderful dream.

She knew she was in love because there was no other emotion she could think of to describe her feelings of elation. As they neared her chambers Sahansan open the door and checked her rooms. Before departing, he reminded her not to leave her rooms until he returned in the morning to escort her downstairs to breakfast. Guards remained posted at her door.

Chapter 10

During the night a courier from the Middle Kingdom arrived with news for Prince Kayan that King Oba was dead. The new King sent the messenger to King Aaron with the news. King Aaron immediately called King Jordan and Sahansan into a secret meeting after he had dismissed the messenger.

King Aaron explained his misgivings about the situation, "King Oba is dead and as we know he had no son of his own. This means Prince Kayan is the new ruler of the Middle Kingdom. And King Jordan, I tell you frankly I do not like this at all. Kayan cannot be trusted!"

"You are right old friend. Our kingdoms have worked well together and we have lived in peace. But Kayan is a greedy and conniving man. The Middle Kingdom will not fare well under his rule," said King Jordan.

"Queen Zara stayed in the Middle Kingdom to

supervise the care of King Oba and I believe that she had a hand in his death." Sahansan quietly put in.

Neither kings looked surprised at his words, they had suspected as much when King Kayan and his party had arrived at the wedding without Princess Zara.

"Let us go and meet with him. He should be in the Ochuc room by now" King Aaron said. The three men walked together towards the Ochuc room, their thoughts were racing.

Chapter 11

Meanwhile, the Sorceress Aza stood upon the deck of an immense vessel which belonged to one of the slave traders. She stood with the wind blowing her black cloak about her, talking with the head captain, outlining the evil plan that King Kayan had whispered to her. The slave traders were to invade the wedding party and capture as many boys and men as they could to take to their Kingdom.

They were in the process of building great monuments and rebuilding various parts of their kingdom. Thousands toiled day and night and many had died from the intense labor and harsh work conditions. There was a constant need for more strong bodied slaves.

The Sorceress had used her magic to make them believe that it would be easy. All sensible thought had left the invaders after she had blown her magic potion upon the winds. It had covered the air that surrounded them, leaving them agreeable to every word she had uttered.

The slave traders did not know that they would be going up against the mighty warriors of the Gold and Salt Kingdoms, as well as seasoned fighters among the guests. They did not have to fear the warriors of the Middle Kingdom. King Kayan's small band of powerful warriors would not be fighting against the slave traders, but with them to overthrow the two kingdoms.

The six ships of slave traders quickly emptied, leaving only enough men necessary to keep the ships safe as they marched heavily armed towards the Gold Kingdom. The Sorceress boldly led the way until they were within a couple of miles of the Gold Kingdom, and then she vanished into the early morning fog.

"Where did she go?" The captains' asked each other.

"It doesn't matter. The villages are straight ahead of us." The leader said.

"You don't think we are being led into a trap?" One

of the captains nervously asked.

There was a roar of laughter, "What, by these half naked savages?"

And the laughter rang out again as the men prepared to break camp and continued their march to what they believed were simple, poorly protected villages in the midst of a huge wedding celebration.

Invisible, Aza made her way to the underground tunnel in one of the gold filled mountains that rose from the earth near the Gold Kingdom. The Sorceress has lived for hundreds of years and she knew the land the way most would know the back of their own hands. With eyes that glowed in the dark, causing her to need no torch, she made her way through the tunnel, coming out near the far wall of the palace not caring who saw her. There was none who could stop her now.

Chapter 12

The sound of the alarm alerted everyone to an enemy attack. King Aaron led men to the weapons' room, where they girded themselves up for battle. Palace guards led the Queens to a secret chamber deep within the palace. Other guards led the other women, children and the elderly into another safe area underground.

Princess Naima hid from the guards and returned to her rooms. Being confined with so many others was not to her liking at all. She could hear the sounds of weeping frighten women and the cries of children rising from somewhere beneath her floors.

She could also hear the sounds of battle, but she could not see the battle, she felt powerless. She wanted to escape her rooms and help her father and her beloved Prince. She stared helplessly from her window.

Just as she was about to turn away from her window she saw a strange sight. A woman wearing a long black cape, with long green and brown unbounded hair and wearing a sheer black and silver gown, making her way to the entrance of one of the kingdom's underground treasuries.

Princess Naima did not recognize the woman, but she recognized the long silver staff that the woman carried and knew that she had to be the banished Sorceress Aza. The last of her kind and the most evil, the Princess knew she must escape her room, so that she could try to stop the Sorceress.

The Princess rapidly explained to Aida the need for her to help get her out of her room and pass the guards at the end of the hallway. The guards guarded the entrance to the passages that hid the Queens. Aida looked at the Princess as though she had lost her mind, to approach the Sorceress would be madness!

Aida pulled free of the Princess' restraining hands and made her way to the door. She was going to tell Queen

Adama. But before she could make it to the door, she sank to the floor unconscious. Princess Naima had hit her mocicha over the head with a vase! She felt horrible about doing it, but she had to escape her chambers.

She hurriedly undressed Aida and put on her clothes. She carefully covered her face and opened the door. Naima walked unhurriedly into freedom under the unsuspecting noses of the guards.

She made her way to the treasure room through an opening behind her father's golden throne. She didn't know what she was going to do. But she knew she had to do something!

Sorceress Aza appeared to be changing gold into moving objects, and she was directing the objects out to the tunnel. *I must stop her*, Naima thought. She slowly made her way around the edges of the room to the entrance. The Princess knew if she caught her unaware she could render her unconscious.

She quietly bent down to pick up a medium sized golden ball from the floor. Unfortunately, she lost her balance and knocked over one of the gold pots that were near the entrance. The Sorceress swung around towards the sound anticipating a warrior. But instead she faced the beautiful Princess Naima!

"Well, well! What do we have here? The Sorceress' derisive question had the desired effect.

Princess Naima was terrified! The look of malice on the Sorceress' face was more intimidating than anything that she had ever seen. Before fear could cause her to lose her nerve, she threw the golden ball at the Sorceress and attempted to run.

But her feet refused to obey her brain's commands! She felt her limbs stiffening. The Princess quickly looked down and saw that her entire body was swiftly turning to gold. She looked toward the entrance and uttered her one last word before she became the Gold Princess, "Zareb"!

Chapter 13

Sahansan was deep in battle fighting off three of the slave traders when he sensed a powerful presence. He turned as he cut down the last man. He saw in the distance the Sorceress Aza making her way to the treasure chambers.

He fought his way through more men as he made his way after her. He stood briefly immobilized with shock as he entered the treasure room. He could scarcely believe his eyes when he saw that the Princess Naima had been turned into a gold statue!

"Enough!" he quickly killed the watery eyed man who had followed him in. He yelled out to the Sorceress Aza, "Old witch you will regret the day you dared to enter the Gold Kingdom!"

Sahansan threw up his hands at the same time the Sorceress aimed her silver staff at him in a vain attempt to turn him into gold. He warded off the spell with an invincible defensive shield that he placed in front of himself.

Out of nowhere lighting shot from Sahansan hands and struck down the evil Sorceress! Her very brief reign of terror had ended. The Sorceress crumbled lifelessly to the floor. The gold and diamond treasures that she had seized, turned and moved back into their places in the treasure room. But not Princess Naima!

She stood glittering and unmovable. And more beautiful than she had ever been, but still solid gold. Sahansan being a good and powerful sorcerer knew that if the spell was not broken before the setting of the evening sun, Princess Naima would remain for all of time locked in her golden prison.

He ran from the cave and called to one of the Gold Kingdom warriors demanding that he, "Guard this gold statue with your life!"

Then Sahansan went in search of King Aaron and

Prince Zareb, because he knew only Prince Zareb had the power to break the spell. The battle had grown quite intense. Men fell to the ground and lay dead and dying. Neither side gave an inch!

Chapter 14

King Kayan, two of his men and several slave traders fought extremely well side by side against King Aaron. The king's diamond and solid gold breast plates and arm bands shielded him against their swords and flying burning balls of iron as they fought.

Sahansan rushed into the midst of the battle, slicing men down as he made his way to a high platform against the courtyard wall. The fighting continued unabated around him. But Sahansan had more pressing matters now, he had no more time to fight with these men!

He stopped when he reached the top of the platform, twirled in a wide circle with his hands outstretched and shouted loudly, "Protect all who stand with the Gold Kingdom!"

Thick gray smoke and a bright blue light shone brightly around all of King Aaron's and King Jordan's warriors and allies. Fear struck the heart of the men at the sight of this great unnatural occurrence. And the fighting ceased immediately!

Everyone turned and looked at Sahansan who continued to speak, "Men from beyond the Seven Seas you cannot hurt us! The Creator is smiling down on us! I do not use magic for evil, but for good. I will not hurt you as long as you turn around and leave and never return to these lands or the neighboring lands again. King Aaron, all of your true friends and allies are protected!"

The blue light flowed around all except the enemies of King Aaron.

"Your highness you see that King Kayan, Prince Chumbe, and their men mean you and your people harm. What do you want me to do with them?" Sahansan asked.

"Who is leading this attack? Step forth or my warriors will slaughter all of you where you stand!" yelled King Aaron.

A tall slender man with dark blonde hair and intense

blue eyes stepped forth and said, "I am Captain Hawk. If you spare me and my men, we will not come to your shores again."

King Aaron said, "First, you will tell me whether or not you were working with that man?" He pointed to King Kayan.

The captain shook his head and said, "I have never seen him before. But the witch who led us here told us the new ruler of the Middle Kingdom have many slaves for sale. We need more slaves to help rebuild our kingdom and to complete the monuments we are building to honor our gods."

"Is that right?" King Aaron said quietly. "Bring that snake forward now!"

The Goldia warriors closest to King Kayan and Prince Chumbe pushed the group forward, closer to the angry king.

"You dare to bring this"... King Aaron angrily

waved his powerful arms around at the scene before him, "to my kingdom! You make deals with slave traders to take my people?! Tell me how is it that this Captain Hawk knew about there being a new ruler of the Middle Kingdom when none of us knew until late last night?"

Before King Kayan could answer, his chief aide, Khalil stepped forward and said loudly and very clearly that Prince Kayan knew because his wife, Princess Zara had poisoned King Oba. Khalil told everyone that could hear his voice how he had seen Princess Zara put poison in King Oba's food.

He also told them how he had quickly located Prince Kayan and had told him what he had seen his wife do to his brother's food. Khalil said he knew that he had made a mistake in telling Prince Kayan when he saw the flash of quickly concealed joy on his face.

Khalil said he later realized after his family had been abducted that he should have gone to the Council of

Twelve instead of to Prince Kayan. He said that Prince Kayan's plans were to take over the Gold and Salt Kingdoms by making sure King Aaron and King Jordan were killed. And, that Prince Kayan meant to have as many men as possible traded to the slave traders in exchange for their weapons of roaring fire.

Khalil dropped to his knees before King Aaron and said, "Forgive me, but he has my wife and three children locked away! He has threatened to kill them if I did not cooperate with him."

Once Khalil had started speaking it was as if a fountain had burst forth from the earth. Silence prevailed as he continued to speak.

"Prince Kayan was behind the attempted kidnapping of Princess Naima. He had planned on using her as bait to trap you, if you had not been killed by the slave traders. He wants your kingdom and King Jordan's kingdom!"

"You sniveling idiot! I killed your wife and three whining brats the day after I imprisoned them!" King Kayan cruelly laughed, "Did you honestly think I was going to waste food and water on that lot?"

He laughed again and spit in Khalil's face. Rage swept through Khalil's tall thin body. He grabbed the weapon of fire from Captain Hawk's hand and pointed it directly at King Kayan and fired! Blood poured out of the gaping hole in King Kayan's chest and he fell to the ground, dead.

Prince Chumbe cried out "No, not my father!"

He looked at Khalil and angrily hissed, "I will get you for this!"

Khalil sadly stared at him and said, "Your father has already gotten me! Everyone that I love is dead." He dropped the weapon and turned his back on Prince Chumbe as tears streamed down his cheeks.

King Aaron turned to Captain Hawk and said, "You

were tricked into attacking us. And when you were told to stop fighting us, you did. You are free to go and you may take Prince Chumbe and the rest of King Kayan's conspirators with you. Mark well my words Captain, do not ever think to come to our lands again, because it will not end so well for you. I assure you of this!"

The invaders quickly left with their new slaves. Sahansan stepped forward and said, "My King, Princess Naima is in grave danger. The Sorceress Aza turned her into a gold statue and the only person that may be able to save her life is King Zareb."

Chapter 15

Upon the death of his father Prince Zareb had become the new King of the Middle Kingdom. Now King Zareb, who had stood quietly listening to all of the accusations against his father without a hint of emotion, did not feel the same calm upon hearing the news of his beloved Naima. His brown skin turned ashen as he felt the blood drain from his face. *Not his beautiful feisty Naima!*

"King Zareb! King Zareb!" He heard King Aaron call his name.

He forced himself to master his emotions as he briefly met King Aaron's worried gaze before turning to look into Sahansan's eyes.

"Tell me what I need to do?" He asked.

"Do you love Princess Naima?" Sahansan asked.

"I love her with all my heart and soul!" He answered.

"Go to her and tell her that and do what comes

naturally." Sahansan commanded.

"What do you mean? Do what?" He questioned in bewilderment.

"The Creator will show you the way. Now go quickly before the sun sets!"

They all turned as one and looked up into the heavens and noticed that the light of day was rapidly fading. King Zareb ran to the opening of the treasure room door and disappeared inside. King Aaron laid down his weapons and knelt in the golden dirt of the palace's outer courtyard.

He lifted his hands upward toward the sky and began to pray to the Creator of Heaven and Earth to save his little princess. All the warriors laid down their weapons and knelt down. With arms outstretched toward the fading blue skies, they silently joined in the King's prayer.

Chapter 16

Inside the treasure room, King Zareb approached the golden statue of Princess Naima and began to tell her how much he loved her. But she remained locked in gold. With tears gathering in his eyes and slowly drifting downward, he leaned forward stroking her golden cheeks. Nothing happened.

He cupped her face between his hands and tenderly kissed her lips. The tears that flowed from his eyes dropped upon her golden cheeks and her eyelids fluttered as she slowly opened her eyes. The noise of the gold dropping to the floor as it flowed from her body was the only sound in the room before King Zareb let out such a loud shout of joy that it was heard by all in the courtyard.

King Aaron and the others came rushing in. Great was the joy of all who saw that Princess Naima was alive and free from the evil sorceress' spell!

King Zareb moved his body closer to hers and said, "I will never let you go! I love you and desire above all things for you to rule by my side. Will you marry me?"

She whispered yes before her lips gently met his in a tender kiss. And, there was another wedding that very week in the Gold Kingdom and they all lived happily ever after.

The End